Knowing and seeing are not the same . . .

"How did you open the terrace door?" Annabel asked.

The cat shrugged, rolling its emerald eyes. "I'm not a real cat."

"I can see that!" Annabel giggled. Imagine a gold toy thinking it was real!

"No you can't. All you see is a cat, and that isn't me at all. On the other hand," said the cat, "when I look at you, I don't see a little girl named Annabel."

Annabel looked down at herself. "If you don't see a little girl," she asked, "then what do you see?"

"A fairy," said the cat.

No
Flying
in the
House

No Flying in the House

by Betty Brock

Illustrated by Wallace Tripp

HarperTrophy®
An Imprint of HarperCollinsPublishers

Library of Congress
Catalog Card Number: 79-104755
ISBN: 0-06-440130-8 (pbk.)

---

13   CG/OPM   30 29 28 27 26 25 24 23
First Harper Trophy edition, 1982
Revised Harper Trophy edition, 2005
Visit us on the World Wide Web!
www.harperchildrens.com

For C.C.,
Leslie,
and Alison

Chapter 1

One morning before breakfast Mrs. Vancourt stepped out on her terrace to look at the ocean. On the stone railing, watching a sea gull fall out of sight below the cliffs, sat a tiny white dog. It was only three inches high and three inches long. Almost hidden under its short white fur was a solid-gold collar engraved with the word *GLORIA*.

"Amazing!" exclaimed Mrs. Vancourt, placing Gloria in her palm. "I thought you were a toy! Are you a puppy?"

The dog's blue eyes, searching her wrinkled face, were calm and clear.

Mrs. Vancourt shook her head. "No, you are definitely not a puppy. But what an incredible specimen. Only three inches high! Do you know any tricks?"

Gloria wagged her short curly tail. "A few," she answered.

Mrs. Vancourt glanced around the terrace. Except for the dog, she was alone.

"It was only the roar of the surf," she told herself. But to make sure, she asked again, "Do you know any tricks?"

This time Gloria answered in a very loud voice, "About three hundred and sixty-seven!"

With a shaking hand, Mrs. Vancourt

put on the glasses hanging from a gold chain around her neck. "You *did* say 'three hundred and sixty-seven,' " she said, looking Gloria right in the eye, "didn't you?"

"Give or take a few," said Gloria.

"Incredible!" said Mrs. Vancourt. "A talking dog!"

"Most people are surprised at first," said Gloria. "If I startled you, I'm sorry."

"I thought I was losing my mind!" said Mrs. Vancourt. "How did you get on my terrace? Are you lost?"

"Not exactly," said Gloria. "As a matter of fact, I just arrived in the neighborhood. I'm looking for a home."

Mrs. Vancourt adored small things. "I suppose a talking dog three inches high and three inches long can pick and choose," she said. "What sort of place are you looking for?"

"I'm not particular," said Gloria. "Three meals a day, cozy fires, fresh flowers, birthday cakes, singing, and laughter."

Mrs. Vancourt laughed. What fantastic luck! In exchange for a few comforts this talented dog could be hers! She carried

Gloria into her elegant drawing room and placed the little dog carefully on a table beside her chair.

"My dear Gloria," she said, "your search is ended. My home is yours for as long as you care to stay!"

Gloria glanced behind her, through the open French doors to the terrace. "It isn't just for me," she said.

At that moment a child appeared in the doorway. She was three years old, with short blond hair and cheeks as soft as fresh raspberries.

"Come in, Annabel," said Gloria. "I want you to meet Mrs. Vancourt. She has kindly offered us a home."

"Not 'us,' " said Mrs. Vancourt quickly as the child approached the table. "Just you, Gloria. Just you. Nothing was said about a child!"

"Annabel Tippens is well behaved," said Gloria.

"No," said Mrs. Vancourt. "Not a child. Not possibly. Not in this house. I'll never agree to it. Never in a million years."

Calmly, Gloria studied Mrs. Vancourt's

determined face. "I couldn't stay without Annabel," she said.

Mrs. Vancourt shook her head. "My house," she said, "is not an orphanage!"

"Annabel is not an orphan," said Gloria. "Due to circumstances beyond their control, her parents left her in my care.

One day they will return. Our stay with you will be only temporary."

Mrs. Vancourt hesitated. She almost never changed her mind. She looked at Annabel and then at Gloria. "Do you really know three hundred and sixty-seven tricks?"

Gloria stood up. She flipped her hind legs into the air and ran around in a circle on her front paws. It was a circus-dog's trick, but she accomplished it with incredible ease. Then she did a couple of backflips and a forward roll.

"More!" cried Annabel, clapping her hands.

Starting with a triple roll, Gloria did all her tricks—jumping, rolling, flying about, her little black nose and paws skimming over the polished table like spots on rolling dice. After trick three hundred and sixty-seven she wasn't even out of breath.

"Now, about Annabel," she said. "Before the sun sets I must find her a home."

In all the capitals of Europe, Mrs. Vancourt had never seen a performance that could compare with this one. She put her glasses on and off a dozen times, trying to make up her mind. She knew that her opportunity to own a live talking dog three inches high and three inches long that did hundreds of tricks might never come again.

"Before the sun sets," repeated Gloria.

Mrs. Vancourt looked at Annabel and forced a smile. Then she picked up Gloria. "Come along then," she said, "it's time for breakfast."

Except for a few servants, Mrs. Vancourt lived alone. Her very large house, surrounded by gardens and smooth lawns, overlooked a wide river where it emptied into the sea. Far out on the horizon a lighthouse stood, like a piece of white chalk against the blue sky.

In the dining room Gloria and Annabel met the plump housekeeper, Miss Peach. Though she had no waist to speak of, Miss Peach moved as briskly as a sergeant major. She carried out Mrs. Vancourt's every wish with military precision, failing only to obey the order to diet. Secretly, Miss Peach carried candy in her pocket.

"A child in the nursery again!" she exclaimed, smiling down at Annabel. Miss Peach was accustomed to Mrs. Vancourt's sometimes unusual guests, who ranged from turbaned maharajas to kimonoed Japanese, and her surprise when Gloria said "How do you do?" registered only in her kind llama-like eyes.

After breakfast Mrs. Vancourt and Miss Peach took Gloria and Annabel up to the old nursery. It was a large plain room with white furniture and a fireplace.

Miss Peach raised the blinds, letting in the bright sunshine. She opened the tall windows and the balcony door to let in the smell of the sea and the roar of the surf breaking against the cliffs below the lawn.

Mrs. Vancourt walked around shaking her head. "This nursery has been closed up for so many years," she said, "it will have to be completely redecorated."

"That won't be necessary," said Gloria. "All we need are some clothes for Annabel. Unfortunately, I was unable to bring her things."

Annabel ran about the nursery, finding

blocks and books, balls and stuffed animals. "A rocking horse!" she cried, climbing aboard. A moment later she spied the
electric train that ran under the little white
bed, and she slid down to investigate. Because she was only three, she didn't notice
that there were no dolls. But Gloria noticed.
Once this nursery had been used by a boy.

Mrs. Vancourt decided to show off her
talented dog that very afternoon.

"Please tell Cook to make some petits
fours," she told Miss Peach. "I want to
have some friends in for tea, to meet my new
pet."

She carried Gloria into the bathroom.
"After I have bathed you, I'm going to re-
place that plain gold collar with a lovely
emerald one."

The hair on Gloria's back bristled, but
when she spoke, her voice was calm. "I am
accustomed to bathing myself," she said.
"Annabel and I take a bath every day."

"How do you turn on the water?" asked
Mrs. Vancourt.

"When Annabel gets stuck, I help her,"

said Gloria. "Together we are very strong. And as for my collar, I prefer it over any other."

"Even for a party?"

Mrs. Vancourt was quite put out, but Gloria refused to change collars. She also refused to speak to the guests.

"You can't refuse!" said Mrs. Vancourt. "I'm counting on it!"

Gloria sighed. "A talking dog would attract too much publicity," she explained. "It isn't good for Annabel. Someday I hope to have a stage career, but it will have to wait until Annabel is older."

Though Mrs. Vancourt was accustomed to getting her own way, she didn't argue. But she was disappointed.

To make it up to her, Gloria did her best trick for the guests. That afternoon when they were gathered in the drawing room, drinking tea and eating Cook's petits fours, Mrs. Vancourt placed Gloria on the mantel.

"Attention, everyone!" she called. "I would like to introduce Gloria. She is going to entertain you."

Gloria walked to the center of the mantel and bowed.

Everyone clapped.

Then while Annabel tapped smartly on a toy drum Gloria dove into space, somersaulting four times in midair before landing without a splash in a bowl of water on the hearth.

Everybody gasped. Then they clapped and clapped, calling out "Encore, encore!" while Gloria bowed. She did all three hundred and sixty-seven tricks. She was a sensation.

"What an act!" cried Mrs. Vancourt. "Eleanor Adams wants to buy you!"

Immediately, she ordered four diamond ankle bracelets as small as baby rings, and a stage no larger than a hatbox, with velvet curtains and hand-painted scenery. Gloria agreed to use them at her next performance.

The next day Gloria went shopping with Mrs. Vancourt for Annabel's clothes. The chauffeur, Charles, drove them into town in a long black limousine. In the department-store crowds, Mrs. Vancourt was so afraid of losing Gloria that she stuffed her into her purse, almost suffocating her.

"Help!" called Gloria the first time the woman opened her purse to ask what size socks Annabel wore. "Let me out! I need air!"

"You could be kidnapped," said Mrs. Vancourt.

The saleswoman stared. "Is that a dog or a toy?" she asked.

Other shoppers gathered around.

Mrs. Vancourt snapped her purse shut. Gloria was smashed between a wallet full of one-hundred-dollar bills and a diamond-studded gold compact.

When the purse opened again, Mrs. Vancourt was standing at a counter covered with purses. "I'm buying a plastic one you can see through," she told Gloria. "The salesgirl is very kindly punching air holes in it. You can't say I don't cooperate."

But when Mrs. Vancourt got on an elevator, carrying Gloria in the new plastic purse, Gloria found herself looking into the round freckled face of a small boy. First he stuck out his tongue. Then he made faces. When he began poking through the holes at her with his fingers, Gloria began to bark.

The people on the elevator stared.

A lady with a large black poodle said, "Pathetic."

When they arrived at the Children's Department, Gloria demanded to be released. "It's undignified," she told Mrs. Vancourt. "Did you see that poodle? He was laughing!"

Mrs. Vancourt opened the purse, but her fear of losing her new dog was so great Gloria finally submitted to a small gold chain on her collar. Even then, Mrs. Vancourt came home a nervous wreck.

Chapter 2

Mrs. Vancourt treated Gloria like a queen. For Gloria's convenience she had the nursery bell lowered. Gloria could ring for anything she needed.

"Her knowledge is fantastic," Mrs. Vancourt told Miss Peach. "Did you know that she can discuss any subject in any language?"

"She won't speak even one language when strangers are around," said Miss Peach. "I asked her a question in front of the grocery boy, and she barked at me!"

"The servants have promised to keep her secret," said Mrs. Vancourt.

"And they will," said Miss Peach. "Everyone loves Gloria. Charles takes her in the car wherever she wants to go. Cook sends up special tidbits after a party. I've been playing checkers with her. She moves the pieces with her mouth."

"Who wins?"

"Gloria."

The little dog's devotion to Annabel was so great that she never allowed her performances to interfere with her care of the child. One afternoon Mrs. Vancourt waited impatiently in the drawing room full of guests for Gloria to appear. At last she sent Miss Peach to the nursery.

"Please hurry," said Miss Peach to Gloria. "Everyone is asking for you."

Gloria shook her head. "Annabel has a fever. Dr. Watkins is on his way over. Tell Mrs. Vancourt I can't leave Annabel."

"But we're entertaining a baroness and a governor!" said Miss Peach.

Gloria refused to leave. "Annabel comes first," she said. "Even if we're entertaining the President, Annabel comes first!"

Gloria taught Annabel to wash behind her ears and to put away her toys. Sitting

on Annabel's shoulder, she read to the child, taught her to play games, and heard her prayers. She took her for walks, swam beside her at the beach, and sat in her lap when she was in the dentist's chair. She even allowed Annabel to dress her in doll clothes and to take her out in a doll carriage.

Mrs. Vancourt became accustomed to having a child in the house. Her visits to the nursery were rare; she never held Annabel in her lap or even held her hand on walks. But when there were no guests, Annabel was permitted to join Mrs. Vancourt and Gloria for afternoon tea by the fire in the sitting room, or for early supper in the great, candlelit dining room.

By the time she was six, because of her association with Gloria, Annabel had developed such respect for small things that Mrs. Vancourt allowed her to enter the drawing room unattended.

It was an elegant room with a crystal chandelier, an Aubusson rug, and antique French furniture. Around the walls, gold-and-glass curio cabinets housed Mrs. Vancourt's famous animal collection. Some of the animals, carved from jade and ivory, were hundreds of years old. Some, like the white mouse with ruby eyes, were enameled and studded with precious jewels. But the most famous were the golden toys made for kings and emperors, with windup keys in their backs to make them move.

Of all the golden toys in Mrs. Vancourt's collection, Annabel's favorite was a gold swan with diamond eyes and an ivory beak. When it was wound up, it spread its wings and stretched its graceful neck in every direction.

Gloria's favorite, a hippopotamus dressed as an organ-grinder, played a tune while a tiny monkey with a ruby collar danced on his shoulder.

Of course, Mrs. Vancourt never let anyone, not even Miss Peach, touch the contents of her cabinets. But it gave her the greatest pleasure to bring out the small jeweled objects of enameled gold for Annabel and Gloria to admire at a respectful distance.

"They're worth a king's ransom," Miss Peach told Annabel, "but she'd swap them all for another like Gloria!"

One rainy afternoon Mrs. Vancourt and Gloria went shopping, leaving Annabel in the care of Miss Peach. While the housekeeper sorted sheets in the linen closet Annabel slipped away and went into the drawing room alone.

Cold shadows crowded the big room, usually so bright on a clear day. Wind-driven rain tapping against the glass doors sounded as though it was trying to invade the house. She could hear the rain dripping down the chimney into the black fireplace. Annabel shivered.

Suddenly, a door from the terrace banged open. A cold wet blast swept into the room. The chandelier tinkled like a wind chime. Annabel put her hand over her mouth.

Out on the terrace the wind and rain slashed about as though they were arguing over which would enter first. The curtains flapped into the room like sails. Gathering her courage, Annabel moved to the door and tried to close it. She battled the curtains. With all her strength she pushed. At last the door closed.

To her surprise, on turning back into the room she saw that the door to one of the gold cabinets had come open. Keeping to the center of the room to avoid the shadowy spots along the walls, Annabel went to close it.

Inside the cabinet her favorite swan held its wings poised as if ready for flight. Annabel knew better than to touch it. Even under Mrs. Vancourt's supervision she had never been allowed so much as to stroke it with a finger.

Glancing around to make sure she was alone, Annabel reached for the tiny swan. Its diamond eyes glittered. It felt strangely cold, not at all as she had supposed its bright-gold body would feel. Wonderingly, she turned it over in her hand. Every part was exquisitely molded, from its ivory beak to its gold, webbed feet.

Carefully, just as she had seen Mrs. Vancourt do, Annabel wound the key in its back. The swan began moving its wings and stretching its neck.

Delighted, Annabel waited for it to stop, then wound it up again. This time just as she lifted her hand from the key she heard a terrible grinding. The swan's neck jerked once and sagged.

Annabel shook it.

Nothing moved. She shook it again. How could it break? She had been so careful, just like Mrs. Vancourt always was. Close to tears, she shoved the swan back into place on its glass shelf and started to close the door.

"Now you'll catch it!" said a small voice, clearly from inside the gold cabinet. "You know Mrs. Vancourt has told you never to touch her things!"

Annabel's first thought was to scream for Miss Peach. Backing away, she realized that since the voice was coming from the cabinet it had to belong to something smaller than she. Bravely, she stepped closer, peering through the open cabinet door. There, crouched on the second shelf in a spot she was sure had previously been empty, was a little enameled-gold cat with emerald eyes.

"Who are you?" Annabel asked. "I don't remember seeing you there before."

The cat swished its golden tail. "I just came in out of the weather," it said.

"How did you open the terrace door?" Annabel remembered it had taken all her strength to close it.

The cat shrugged, rolling its emerald eyes. "I'm not a real cat."

"I can see that!" Annabel giggled. Imagine a gold toy thinking it was real!

"No you can't. All you see is cat, and that isn't me at all. On the other hand," said the cat, "when I look at you, I don't see a little girl named Annabel."

Annabel looked down at herself. "If you don't see a little girl," she asked, "then what *do* you see?"

"A fairy," said the cat.

Shaking her head, Annabel laughed. "You don't make sense."

The cat smiled, swishing its tail again. "Neither do you."

Annabel leaned closer. "But I'm not a fairy!"

"You're Annabel Tippens, aren't you?" asked the cat.

Annabel nodded. How did it know her name?

"And Princess Felicia's dog, Gloria,

is your guardian?"

"Who is Princess Felicia?" asked Annabel.

The cat sniffed irritably. "Don't you know anything? For a fairy you're terribly dull!"

"But I'm not a fairy!" insisted Annabel. "Do you know Gloria?"

The cat laughed—rather an evil laugh, Annabel thought.

"I suppose you're going to tell me Gloria isn't a dog!" exclaimed Annabel.

The cat yawned. "You're brighter than I thought."

This time it was Annabel's turn to laugh. "If Gloria isn't a dog, she would have told me. You're terribly mixed up. To get straight, you should admit to yourself right off that you're a cat! A toy one, I mean. Cats are really very nice. I like cats."

"You're only saying that because you don't want me to tell Mrs. Vancourt about the swan."

For the moment Annabel had forgotten the swan.

"I can fix it," said the cat. "If you promise

not to tell the household of my visit today, I'll fix the swan so Mrs. Vancourt will never know it was broken."

Annabel wasn't sure she should trust the cat. But she had no choice. "If only you could!"

"Do you promise?"

She promised gratefully.

"Don't forget," said the cat. "If you ever tell anyone in the house of my visit, that swan will immediately break into one thousand five hundred and sixty-seven pieces."

Annabel didn't want to think about it. "I won't forget," she said.

"Now," said the cat, "you'd better be getting back to the nursery before you're missed. Leave the cabinet door ajar. I'll close it as I leave."

"You're going out? I didn't think cats liked storms!"

"They don't."

"Excuse me." Annabel smiled. "I forgot you aren't a cat. Will you be coming back?"

Offended, the cat sniffed. "Perhaps. When you're old enough to hold an *intelligent* conversation." Turning its back on

Annabel, the cat refused to say another word.

All the way upstairs, Annabel wished she had asked the cat more questions. On the landing, she started to return, but Miss Peach called her to the nursery. "I'll bring you a cup of chocolate and read you a story," she promised.

Annabel chose her favorite book, and when she was comfortably arranged in Miss Peach's lap, she opened it to the first story.

Miss Peach smiled at the pictures. "This was Tommy's favorite too," she said.

"Was Tommy Mrs. Vancourt's son?" asked Annabel. For as long as she could remember, she had seen hanging in the stair hall a large portrait of Mrs. Vancourt's husband, who had died many years ago. A boy leaned against his knee. Once when she questioned Gloria about this, the little dog cautioned her about prying into matters that were none of her business.

"He was her only son," said Miss Peach.

"Is he the one in the picture?"

Miss Peach nodded. "We don't mention him outside the family, and never in front of Mrs. Vancourt. He ran away." She shook her head sadly. "No trace of him was ever found. This room was his nursery."

Annabel had guessed as much. "When did he run away?"

"Long ago. He was almost grown-up." Miss Peach shook her head. "Left in the middle of the night. Poor dear, always believing his mother loved those golden toys in the drawing room more than she loved him."

"Didn't she?"

Miss Peach clucked like an excited hen. "Mrs. Vancourt adored the boy! But you know how she is about those toys. The night he left, he broke her favorite. Though it was an accident, she was wildly angry. You know she never lets anyone touch her things."

Annabel nodded guiltily, hoping the swan was now repaired. She hated to think what Mrs. Vancourt would do if she discovered it was broken. "Which one did he break?" she asked.

"It isn't there anymore," said Miss Peach. "When Tommy left, he took the pieces with him." She smiled a sad little smile and offered Annabel a peppermint from her pocket. "I can still remember its emerald eyes glittering there on the floor among the broken pieces."

"Was it a pretty one?"

Miss Peach nodded. "The prettiest, I thought. In fact, it was my favorite too."

"Did it wind up?"

"Oh my, yes. It even swished its tail. It was a fancy one."

Annabel sat up. She shivered. "Its tail?" she whispered. "What sort of toy was it?"

Seeing her shiver, Miss Peach felt Annabel's forehead. "Don't tell me you're catching a cold, with school starting a week from Tuesday!"

"Please, Miss Peach," begged Annabel. "Was it a cat?"

"A good guess," said Miss Peach. "It was indeed a cat. A little golden cat with emerald eyes."

Chapter 3

The moment Gloria and Mrs. Vancourt returned, Gloria began to sniff. She sniffed all through the house, all the way up to the nursery.

"Have we had callers this afternoon, Miss Peach?" she asked, sniffing around the window overlooking the wet, darkening garden.

"On an afternoon like this? Not even the grocery boy has come," said Miss Peach. "Cook is fussing."

Annabel, under the bed with the train, was glad they didn't ask her. When she came out to try on her new school dresses that Mrs. Vancourt and Gloria had bought, she noticed Gloria began to sniff harder, but the little dog didn't say what she smelled.

Questions were going off inside Annabel's head like popcorn. Every time she opened her mouth to ask one, she remembered the swan and her promise to the golden cat. No matter how many different ways she turned her questions around in her head, she couldn't decide on a way to ask Gloria about the cat without telling the secret.

Immediately after dinner Annabel ran ahead of Gloria to the drawing room. She had to know if the swan had been fixed. Entering the room, she sensed that something was different. The golden toys, reflecting the firelight like small beacons, appeared to be at attention, listening. Hurrying to the swan's shelf, she saw that its head no longer sagged. It sat poised, ready for flight. The cat had kept its promise. But the spot where the cat had been was empty!

Gloria was sniffing more than ever as she and Mrs. Vancourt came into the room.

"Before you go to bed, Gloria," said Mrs. Vancourt, "you should take a good hot bath. All that sniffing sounds as though you've caught cold. I'll have Miss Peach send you up a toddy."

"Thank you," said Gloria, "but I'm quite well. There is a strange smell in the house tonight. I'm not sure what it is, but I don't like it."

"Probably the onions Cook put in with the roast," said Mrs. Vancourt. Stooping, she picked up something from the floor. With a strange, puzzled look, she turned it over in her hand. "How very odd."

Annabel ran to look. She drew back when she saw that Mrs. Vancourt held a piece of enameled gold studded with an emerald. Was it from the swan? She didn't remember a piece missing, but it could have fallen off unnoticed.

Mrs. Vancourt stared at the piece in her hand. "A fragment from my collection!" She turned it over. "Impossible, unless— Gloria! Do you suppose we could have had a burglar?"

A sweeping glance around the room assured her that nothing appeared to be missing. "Ring for Miss Peach. I want the house searched at once. From basement to attic!"

Then, one by one, Mrs. Vancourt removed her treasures from their glass shelves for examination.

With fingers crossed, Annabel watched Mrs. Vancourt wind up the swan. Its diamond eyes glittered. After one quick jerk it worked perfectly. Annabel smiled, too relieved to wonder how the cat had managed to repair it.

"No sign of the burglar," reported Miss Peach at the end of the search. "Only some cold salmon missing from the refrigerator, and Cook thinks one of the gardeners may have eaten it for lunch."

Annabel wondered if a cat that thought it was something else would eat cold salmon.

"False alarm," admitted Mrs. Vancourt, staring at the fragment of enameled gold in her hand. In the firelight the emerald glowed like a living eye.

Seeing it for the first time, Miss Peach sucked in a frightened gasp. Then she came closer.

"After all these years!" she said, shaking her head.

Mrs. Vancourt held the piece up for her examination. "It's the only explanation," she said. Turning, she spoke to Gloria and Annabel. "Long ago, here in this room, a piece of my collection was broken. It was a little golden cat with emerald eyes. This is a fragment. Do you agree, Miss Peach?"

"There is no doubt about it," said Miss Peach. "In the sweeping up, the piece must have caught in the floorboards. Incredible. I've vacuumed this room myself."

For the rest of the evening a sad half-smile lurked on Mrs. Vancourt's face. Annabel walked around the room with her while she closed all the cabinets. When Mrs. Vancourt came to the one where the cat had been that afternoon, she opened a drawer underneath it, carefully placing the fragment she had found inside on the velvet lining.

That night Annabel dreamed of jigsaw puzzles that became cats and of cats that became jigsaw puzzles.

No more was said about the piece of gold. For a few days Gloria was on edge, jumping at any unusual sound. But she stopped sniffing. At every opportunity, especially on rainy days, Annabel checked the gold cabinets in the drawing room, but the spot on the shelf previously occupied by the cat remained empty.

Even though the cat didn't return, Annabel kept remembering their conversation and wondering who Princess Felicia was and why the cat had wanted her to think she was a fairy. The more she thought, the more the idea of being a fairy appealed to her.

"If I were a fairy, I'd be able to fly, wouldn't I?" Annabel asked Miss Peach one day.

"In my opinion," said Miss Peach, "that's the best part of being a fairy."

"Would I need wings?"

"Not necessarily," said Miss Peach. "But wings would undoubtedly help."

After that, when no one was looking, Annabel practiced flying. She started by jumping off the terrace.

"It should be well in time to start school," said Dr. Watkins when he came to bandage up her ankle. "Next time you decide to go flying, young lady, I suggest you wear your parachute."

Annabel realized the cat had mistaken her for someone else.

By the time school opened, she had forgotten about the cat. The first day, Gloria went with her on the school bus that stopped at the back gate and guided her to Miss Clemments's first-grade class, down the hall from the cafeteria.

Annabel was the only one who brought a pet to school, but everybody thought it was such a wonderful idea that Miss Clemments promised to plan a Pet Day very soon. "In the meantime," she said kindly, "Gloria will have to stay at home."

Even though Gloria did every trick she knew, Miss Clemments shook her head. "The Board of Education won't allow it."

The second morning, Annabel held Gloria in her arms and rubbed her cheek against Gloria's soft white fur. She knew Gloria was very upset at having to stay home. "If only I could tell Miss Clemments you aren't an ordinary dog. You're smart enough to teach that whole school all by yourself."

"Exactly what I pointed out to Mrs. Vancourt," said Gloria candidly. "I told her I could tutor you. But she's against it. In fact, she put her foot down."

When the bus came, Annabel kissed Gloria good-bye and climbed aboard. Gloria sat in the driveway, whimpering until the bus disappeared around a bend. After that, every morning Gloria waited with Annabel by the gate, and every afternoon she watched from a window for Annabel's return. It was as though she were afraid the child was threatened by some secret danger.

At school Annabel's best friend was Beatrice Cox. She and Beatrice were partners for everything, and Miss Clemments even had to change their seats so they wouldn't talk.

One of the first things Annabel found out about Beatrice was that she had a cat.

"She's a genuine Persian," said Beatrice proudly. "With papers."

"Can she talk?" asked Annabel.

"You're kidding," said Beatrice.

"What color?"

"Gold," said Beatrice. "She's very rare."

"Real gold with emerald eyes?" Annabel was excited. "Are you sure she can't talk?"

"Why don't you ask her?" suggested Beatrice. "My mother knows Mrs. Vancourt. She says you can come home with me after school any afternoon."

When Gloria heard Annabel was going home on the bus with Beatrice Cox, she became so upset Mrs. Vancourt had to speak to her.

"The child needs friends her age," explained Mrs. Vancourt. "Even though she loves you dearly, you can't be her whole life. That is why I insisted she go to school. You must not stand in her way."

Gloria lay with her paws over her eyes. "You don't understand," she said. "I have to be with her always. It is my duty."

"No one can say you don't do your duty," said Mrs. Vancourt. "Whoever her parents are, they should be very proud of you. But the child needs some freedom."

In spite of Mrs. Vancourt's advice, Gloria was waiting on Beatrice Cox's front steps when she and Annabel got off the school bus.

"Now how did that dog know you were going to be here?" asked Mrs. Cox while she served them milk and cookies at the kitchen table. "That's a smart pup!"

Annabel nodded, cuddling Gloria on her shoulder.

Even Beatrice didn't know Gloria could talk. Annabel loved Gloria too much to tell her secret. She loved Gloria more than anyone in the world, but she couldn't help envying Beatrice. Mrs. Cox was the first real mother Annabel had ever observed, and she liked the way Mrs. Cox swept Beatrice up into her arms and kissed her. It was impossible to imagine Mrs. Vancourt sweeping anyone up for a kiss, even her own little boy. Annabel wondered how it felt.

They looked for Beatrice's cat up in her room and behind the garage, in her father's vegetable garden and across the street in a vacant field of high grass and goldenrod, where they pretended they were on an African safari, stalking a lion.

When they found the cat asleep on top of the piano, Annabel tried to hide her disappointment. She knew Beatrice was proud of that cat even though it was plain yellow with green eyes and, in spite of its papers, quite ordinary.

Just before Annabel had to leave, Mr. Cox came home. He swung Beatrice up in the air and between his legs, and he hugged and kissed her. Then he hugged and kissed Mrs. Cox. Unaccustomed to fathers, Annabel watched, turning warm inside the way she did on cold days when she drank hot chocolate. Mothers and fathers, she decided, were very nice.

Then, unexpectedly, Mr. Cox swept Annabel up, swinging her just the way he swung Beatrice.

Gloria barked.

Annabel shrieked with delight. It felt wonderful.

When Gloria saw that Annabel liked it, she stopped barking and even wagged her tail.

Before supper Mr. Cox drove them home. He said he considered it an honor that Gloria preferred to ride all the way on his shoulder, and he pretended he was teaching her to drive. Annabel smiled. She knew Mr. Cox wouldn't believe her if she told him Gloria knew everything.

Chapter 4

Until she made friends with Beatrice Cox, Annabel had never thought much about her parents. According to Gloria, someday they would return. In the meantime the little dog gave her a mother's devotion. But after meeting the Coxes, Annabel secretly hoped her parents would be like Mr. and Mrs. Cox.

The first time Beatrice came to play, Annabel took her into the drawing room to see Mrs. Vancourt's animal collection. Standing before the cabinet where she had seen the golden cat, she wished she could tell Beatrice of its visit. After all, Beatrice was her best friend. The golden swan glittering on its shelf reminded her of her promise to keep the cat's visit a secret. It would break into one thousand five hundred and sixty-seven pieces if she told anyone in the household. Suddenly she realized that did not include Beatrice.

"When you look at me, Beatrice," asked Annabel, "what do you see?"

Beatrice looked her up and down. "A girl."

Excited, Annabel twirled around. "Look hard."

"How can I if you don't stand still?" Beatrice looked again. "There's dirt on your dress."

"Is that all?"

"There's some on your face too."

Disappointed, Annabel sighed. "Can you keep a secret?"

Beatrice nodded. "Most of the time. Unless somebody offers me a chocolate bar. I can't stand passing up a chocolate bar."

Willing to take the risk, Annabel told her about the cat's visit. Telling somebody at last gave her a delicious feeling, but when Beatrice began shaking her head, Annabel wished she hadn't shared the secret.

"It said I looked like a fairy!" she insisted.

Beatrice grinned. "You know, Annabel, sometimes I dream about things like that cat. They seem so real I believe they really happened."

Annabel stamped her foot. "Just because you're six months older doesn't mean you know everything. This did happen. It was real!"

Beatrice shrugged. "You look like a plain ordinary girl to me. Anyway, Tippens doesn't sound like a fairy name."

Annabel hesitated. "My mother and father would have to be fairies too, wouldn't they?" She was disappointed that they couldn't be like Mr. and Mrs. Cox.

"By this time wouldn't you have some sign?" asked Beatrice. "Some magic something to make you different? Can you fly?"

"Not even an inch," admitted Annabel.

"Maybe later on you'll grow wings," said Beatrice kindly. "Have you tried recently? To fly, I mean. Jump off that chair."

Annabel shook her head. "It's no use. I've jumped off lots of chairs. The first time, when I jumped off the terrace, I sprained my ankle." She sighed. "If you have to fly to be a fairy, I'm definitely not one."

"How about disappearing?" asked Beatrice. "If you can't fly, maybe you can disappear."

"I thought of that," said Annabel, "but I don't know how. I've even stopped getting lost."

Standing back, Beatrice looked her over critically. "It could be that you just don't know the magic words. If you were little when your parents left you, maybe you were too little to learn fairy secrets."

Annabel brightened. "Do you suppose that's it?"

"Gloria would know," said Beatrice. She didn't know Gloria could talk. She began to giggle. "Why don't you ask Gloria?" The idea of talking with Gloria doubled Beatrice over with laughter.

Annabel didn't laugh. "Maybe I will," she said quietly. But she had to figure out some way to ask Gloria without giving away her secret conversation with the golden cat.

Out in the garden, the girls found Mrs. Vancourt cutting chrysanthemums. She liked Beatrice enough to let her hold the flower basket.

"My father has a garden, and he lets me help him dig," said Beatrice.

"That's a different kind of garden," said Mrs. Vancourt. "However, if you really want to dig, the old larkspur bed by the summerhouse needs to be spaded up."

Annabel brought the shovels, and Mrs. Vancourt showed them where to put a foot on a shovel to push it into the soft earth.

"You may unearth a buried treasure," Mrs. Vancourt said. "Many years ago, Vikings sailed up this river; they may have camped on this very spot."

The girls leaned on the shovels, watching the sharp edges bite into the brown earth. It was hard work. Shortly, they grew tired.

Beatrice kicked at a large clod. "Here's a Viking tin can," she said, holding up her rusty find.

Both girls giggled.

Annabel picked up another clod.

"Here's a Viking rock," she said. She and Beatrice laughed until they doubled up and dropped the shovels.

"Just a minute, smarties," said Mrs. Vancourt, holding out her hand. "Let me see that can. There is something inside."

Annabel and Beatrice stopped laughing. Handing Mrs. Vancourt the can, they heard it rattle. The partially opened end had been pushed in, concealing the contents. Using her garden shears, Mrs. Vancourt pried open the lid.

When she saw what rolled out into Mrs. Vancourt's hand, Annabel gasped.

"What is it?" asked Beatrice.

Looking as though she might cry, Mrs. Vancourt turned over the handful of enameled-gold pieces she held. In one small piece blinked an emerald. "It's a cat," she said, "or what used to be a cat. My little boy broke it long ago. He must have buried the pieces here in the garden."

"Like the cat you saw in the drawing room?" Beatrice asked Annabel, forgetting her promise to keep a secret.

Mrs. Vancourt looked down at Anna-

bel. "You saw a cat like this, Annabel?"

Staring at the pieces of gold in Mrs. Vancourt's hand, Annabel felt sick. Slowly, she shook her head. "I must have dreamed it," she said. "There is no cat now. Only pieces. It must have been a dream."

Annabel didn't feel like playing in the garden anymore. She and Beatrice followed Mrs. Vancourt back to the drawing room and watched her place the gold pieces in the small drawer with the fragment she had found earlier.

"Someday a goldsmith may be able to put the pieces together again," she said.

"Like Humpty Dumpty," Beatrice said, laughing. But Annabel didn't feel like laughing.

Because she liked Beatrice, Mrs. Vancourt wound up several of the golden toys. Even when she wound up the golden swan, Annabel didn't feel any better. She was glad when Beatrice decided to go home early.

"I'm sorry about your secret," said Beatrice before leaving. "It just popped out."

Annabel shrugged. "It doesn't matter. If that cat was buried years ago, I must have dreamed the other one, like you said."

"Could there be two?" asked Beatrice.

Annabel hadn't thought of that. "I don't know," she said. "I'm all mixed up. Right now I don't know what to think."

After she waved good-bye to Beatrice, Annabel climbed the stairs to the nursery.

Miss Peach was leaving. "I just drew a bath for Gloria," she said. "Have you been digging? You'd better take one too."

Through the half-open bathroom door Annabel could hear Gloria singing. Gloria always sang in the tub. Annabel wished she hadn't promised the cat to keep its visit a secret. Of course if there *was* no cat, she could tell Gloria everything. Was there or wasn't there? Surely her memory of breaking the swan was too vivid to be a dream. But if she broke it, who fixed it?

In despair, Annabel sat down on the edge of the bed. Beside her on the coverlet lay Gloria's gold collar. She had seen it each day for as long as she could remember, a gold circle engraved with the name *GLORIA*. Carelessly, Annabel slipped it over her finger, sliding it up and down like a ring. When she was younger, she had seen engraving inside, which she couldn't read except for the word *GLORIA*. She knew that word long before going to school. Now she held the collar up to the light.

In Miss Clemments's first grade she had learned quite a few words. Gloria was teaching her others and how to sound out long ones. Squinting at the small letters, Annabel recognized the word *GLORIA*. There were also some small words. *"To Gloria,"* she read, *"with—love—from"—* it was a hard word. Annabel sounded it out *—"Fe-li-ci-a. With love from Felicia!"*

So Gloria *was* Princess Felicia's dog! "And the cat wasn't a dream!" she said aloud. This proved it. For Annabel to know about Felicia, the cat had to be real.

Chapter 5

Now that Annabel knew that the golden cat had really visited her and it wasn't a dream, she wondered how much of what the cat had said was the truth. It knew her name and that Gloria was her guardian. It knew about Princess Felicia, whoever she might be, and had suggested that Gloria might not be a dog. Of course Annabel knew the cat was all mixed up about her, but it could be right about Gloria. Anybody who really knew Gloria knew she wasn't an ordinary dog.

One day when Annabel was in Mrs. Vancourt's room, watching her sort through her jewel case, she asked her opinion.

"Good heavens, what else could Gloria be if she isn't a dog?" said Mrs. Vancourt.

"She certainly looks like a dog!"

"But she doesn't act like one," said Annabel. "Not a real one."

With a sigh, Mrs. Vancourt held a large ruby ring up to the light. "Gloria is different," she admitted. "But you've always known that. Still, she *is* a dog."

Mrs. Vancourt let Annabel put the ruby ring back in the jewel case. Knowing that one mistake would expel her from Mrs. Vancourt's room forever, she was very careful. "Do you think Gloria could be enchanted?" she asked.

Mrs. Vancourt frowned. "Gloria has never favored me with the story of her past. It's none of my business. Even if she is enchanted, what difference does it make?"

Annabel couldn't tell Mrs. Vancourt about the cat. "If Gloria is my guardian, maybe I'm enchanted too."

Trying on an emerald necklace, Mrs. Vancourt smiled at herself in the mirror. "That makes sense," she admitted. "Do you feel enchanted?"

Annabel thought about it. "I'm not sure what it feels like to be enchanted."

"Stick out your tongue."

Annabel stuck it out.

Peering at it through her glasses, Mrs. Vancourt shook her head. "I think we'd better have Dr. Watkins take a look at you. You may need a tonic. In the meantime, I'll suggest to Miss Peach and Gloria that they stop reading all those fairy tales to you. Better switch to animal stories for a while—dogs or horses. Too many fairy tales could make even *me* feel enchanted."

The next day Miss Peach took Annabel to see Dr. Watkins. As much as he admired Gloria, Dr. Watkins didn't allow dogs in his office.

"I've thought of eliminating mothers, guardians, and nursemaids," said Dr. Watkins, "but then who would do the complaining? Imagine a six-year-old boy telling me to give him medicine because he doesn't drink his milk!"

Annabel liked Dr. Watkins. Secretly she welcomed the examination, for she was sure if there was anything unusual about her, the doctor would find it.

She was weighed and measured. He

didn't even blink when she stuck out her tongue. He looked in her ears and thumped her knees and listened to her chest, front and back, with his stethoscope.

"That's odd," he said finally, removing his stethoscope from her back.

"What's odd?" asked Annabel quickly. "Is something wrong?"

"This little mark on your back. I hadn't noticed it before. Looks like a birthmark."

Annabel twisted her neck around as far as she could. "What little mark?"

"It isn't important," said the doctor. "Lots of people have birthmarks. Yours is unusually pretty."

Standing in front of a mirror, Annabel could just barely see the tiny mark on her shoulder blade.

"Looks like a tiny F with a crown over it," said the doctor.

"I've never seen it before," said Annabel. But she had never examined her back before.

"Probably go away as you grow," said the doctor. "That kind usually does."

Annabel was so anxious to get home to

tell Gloria about the mark on her back she declined Miss Peach's offer of an ice-cream soda.

"It isn't big enough to see without glasses," Miss Peach told Gloria as Annabel undressed to show it to her. "The child is excited about nothing."

Gloria was sitting in the big chair by the fire.

"It's an *F*," said Annabel when Miss Peach was gone. "I'll lean down so you can see it."

"That isn't necessary," said Gloria calmly. "I've seen the mark before. You've always had it. Lots of people have birthmarks."

"But it's an *F*," insisted Annabel.

"Yes."

Annabel took a deep breath. "Is the *F* for Felicia?" she asked.

Very quietly, Gloria motioned for Annabel to sit beside her. "Who told you about Felicia?"

Annabel remembered that the swan would break into one thousand five hundred and sixty-seven pieces if she told. "I saw it in your collar," she said quickly. "I can read just enough to know that it says 'To Gloria, with love from Felicia.' So you must have belonged to her."

After a moment, Gloria nodded. "Yes," she said.

Annabel waited, but she could see

Gloria had nothing more to say. Disappointed, she started to cry. "If you belonged to Felicia, then I must have too. I have her mark on my back."

Quickly Gloria jumped to Annabel's shoulder, comforting her and rubbing soft white fur against her tears. "Don't cry, dearest Annabel," soothed Gloria. "The mark is where Felicia kissed you when you were born. She loved us both very much."

"But who is she?" asked Annabel. "Please, Gloria, tell me about Felicia."

Gloria dropped her eyes sadly. "Felicia's story is part of the past, which for the present must remain a secret. Trust me, my dear. This secrecy is for your own protection. Someday all will be revealed to you. For now, promise to ask me no more questions about Felicia." Again Gloria rubbed her soft fur against Annabel's cheek as if she understood how difficult a request this must be. Only Annabel's respect for Gloria made it possible for her to remain silent.

In the next week a flood of questions tumbled through Annabel's head. Who was Felicia? Why couldn't Gloria talk about her? The golden cat had called her a princess. Princess of what? Could she be Annabel's mother? And if so, did that make Annabel a princess too?

The answer to all her questions lay in pieces in a drawer. Or did it? If the cat had been broken and buried years ago, Annabel reasoned, how had it talked to her?

She decided to continue her search for the golden cat. Each time Mrs. Vancourt and Gloria went shopping, Annabel begged to go along. Amused by her interest, Mrs. Vancourt let her dawdle before jewelry-store windows and department-store gift counters. She took her to beautiful antique shops with carpeting on the floors and to dusty barnlike places where everything lay in piles along the walls.

"I declare, that child is a born shopper!" exclaimed Miss Peach one day when she accompanied them, as she watched Annabel sort through a table of odds and ends. "What can she see in all that junk?"

Annabel saw lots of cats. China cats and wooden cats and bronze cats—even calico cats. But never the golden cat with emerald eyes.

One afternoon in the older part of town near the wharf, where in summer neat little houses trailed petunias from their window boxes, a shop's sign attracted Annabel.

CATTES'S CRANNY
ANTIQUES—OBJECTS D'ART

Announced by a jangling bell, they entered as Mr. Cattes appeared from a back room.

Though he knew Mrs. Vancourt, he eyed Annabel suspiciously. Accustomed to suspicious shopkeepers, Annabel walked about with her hands behind her back. When he saw she wasn't touching things, Mr. Cattes fished a lollipop from a Chinese vase.

"And one for the little dog," he said, handing her one for Gloria, who was perched on Annabel's shoulder.

While Mr. Cattes wound up a gold toy crocodile with ivory teeth for Mrs. Vancourt, Gloria and Annabel explored the shop. The neat front room opened into dusty storerooms cluttered with books, furniture, and glass.

Hopping down from Annabel's shoulder, Gloria began sniffing in a corner stacked with china. Remembering how Gloria had sniffed on the rainy day of the cat's visit, Annabel stood still.

Suddenly Gloria froze. With her head lifted, her little ears stiff, she sniffed deeply.

"What is it?" whispered Annabel.

Gloria shook her head. "Probably a rat," she said. "They're a nuisance in these old houses near the wharf."

Disappointed, Annabel left Gloria poking about the dusty plates to climb a narrow iron staircase, spiraling up to the next floor. She found herself in a long attic strewn with dusty picture frames and broken furniture. At one end, under a high cobweb-draped window, she discovered a doll-house. Part of its roof was missing, the wallpaper hung in shreds, and dust blanketed the furniture. Reaching in to right an overturned doll chair, Annabel's hand almost filled the living room. She blew the dust off the tiny grand piano.

Suddenly, as though the whole doll-house were alive, it began to shake and rock. Puffs of dust rose through its chimney like smoke. At the sound of coughing and sneezing, Annabel leaned down for a closer look.

"You again!" said a voice from inside the dollhouse.

Annabel's mouth fell open. The cat, all in one glittering golden piece, was perched on a stool in the corner of the dollhouse living room.

"Must you make such a mess?" asked the cat. "I can hardly see through this dust, much less breathe!"

Delighted to find the cat at last, Annabel forgot her mouth was open.

"Don't show me your tonsils," said the cat. "Hasn't Gloria told you staring is impolite? You must be terribly stupid."

Annabel snapped her mouth shut. "You're rude," she said indignantly. "I'm not so stupid that I can't see that!"

"Knowing and seeing aren't the same," said the cat.

"I know I see you," said Annabel, "and this time I know you aren't a dream."

"I can be a dream if I like," said the cat.

"Nobody can be a dream," said Annabel. "You're only saying that to show off."

The cat swished its tail. "*I* can."

"If you think so, then you're mistaken.

Just as you were mistaken about my being a fairy. I'm definitely not a fairy. I can't fly."

The cat smiled. "Can you kiss your elbow?"

Annabel looked at the cat suspiciously. She had never tried. "What if I can?" she asked.

The cat yawned. "Then you're a fairy. Only fairies can kiss their elbows."

"Who says!" scoffed Annabel. She turned up her elbow and kissed it easily, right on the point. "There! You see? Anybody can do it."

In the dim light, the cat's emerald eyes began to glitter like sparks from a rocket's tail.

Downstairs, Gloria began to bark.

"Don't move around," said Annabel. "I have some questions to ask." She leaned closer to the dollhouse. "Now where are you going? Do come back. I want to know about Felicia!"

But the cat had left. A puff of dust rose from the corner where it had sat.

"Please!" called Annabel, pushing aside doll tables and moving doll chairs.

"Please, come back!" Her disappointment at having lost the golden cat again was so great she wanted to cry.

Down below, Gloria's barking quickened. Annabel descended the spiral stairs, hoping to find Gloria cornering the cat. Instead, the little dog stood stiff-legged, barking at a mousehole.

"Get back to Mrs. Vancourt," shouted Gloria between barks. "You're in danger!"

"From a mouse?" Reluctantly, Annabel headed toward the front of the shop.

Mrs. Vancourt, hands over her ears, sat watching Mr. Cattes wrap her package.

"Gloria saw a mouse," Annabel explained.

"Very unusual," said Mr. Cattes. "My Tabitha keeps the mice away."

"You have a cat?" Annabel asked quickly. "A gold cat with emerald eyes?"

"That kind couldn't catch a mouse," said Mr. Cattes. "That kind sits on a shelf and yawns when it's wound up. My Tabitha is as gray as a morning mist."

"But the other kind, the kind that sits on a shelf, you have one?"

Mr. Cattes shrugged. "Let's say I *had* one. Bought it at an auction last Saturday. Mrs. Vancourt, I had you in mind. It was a lovely piece of work. Somehow I've misplaced it. Looked high and low."

"What a shame," said Mrs. Vancourt. "My cat was broken, you know."

"Sooner or later this one will turn up," said Mr. Cattes. "I'll save it for your next visit."

Annabel couldn't wait till then. Stepping up to the counter, she said, "Please call instead. I'm very interested in cats."

In a few moments the barking stopped. Looking worried, Gloria joined them, but all the way home in the car she jumped about, sniffing, until Mrs. Vancourt told her that if she didn't stop, next time she would be left at home. Gloria sat looking out the rear window as though she expected something or someone to follow.

Chapter 6

At school the next day Annabel told Beatrice about meeting the cat again.

"Are you sure?" asked Beatrice, trying very hard not to laugh. Though she didn't believe Annabel's stories about the cat, she didn't want to say so.

"Would I tell my best friend a story?" asked Annabel. "That cat was as real as you are. Gloria's barking frightened it away."

"You're sure it talks?" asked Beatrice.

Annabel nodded. "Plain as day. But it doesn't always make sense. It said I was a fairy if I could kiss my elbow. Can you kiss your elbow, Beatrice?"

Beatrice shrugged. "I've never tried." She turned her arm in every direction. "No," she said. "Can you?"

Annabel turned her elbow up and kissed it. "I thought everybody could. Do you suppose that makes me a fairy?"

Beatrice laughed. She couldn't help it.

"The cat said it did," insisted Annabel. "I couldn't sleep last night for thinking about it."

Beatrice smiled, shaking her head. "Anybody can see you're not a fairy, Annabel! Who ever heard of a fairy as big as you? You want to ask Miss Clemments what she thinks? Even if she doesn't know about fairies, she ought to know about elbows."

They found Miss Clemments finishing her lunch in the cafeteria.

"Sure, I can kiss my elbow," joked Miss Clemments. "I can also jump over the moon."

"It's impossible!" gasped Beatrice.

"No, it isn't," insisted Annabel quietly. "Beatrice can't kiss her elbow," she explained to Miss Clemments, "but I can." She didn't tell Miss Clemments about being a fairy.

Miss Clemments stopped laughing. "Show me," she said.

"It's easy," said Annabel, demonstrating.

Miss Clemments shook her head. "You must be very limber or double-jointed," she said. "That's quite a trick."

"Is it different to be double-jointed?" asked Beatrice.

"No. Lots of people are double-jointed," said Miss Clemments. "But Annabel is the only girl I've ever met who could kiss her elbow."

Annabel and Beatrice spent the rest of

recess asking the other children if they could kiss their elbows.

"Even if you're the only one," said Beatrice, "that doesn't make you a fairy."

Annabel wasn't so sure. As usual that afternoon when she got off the bus, Gloria waved to her from an upstairs window. Without stopping in the kitchen for a snack, Annabel ran up to the nursery, where Miss Peach and Gloria were playing checkers by the fire.

Gloria jumped up on Annabel's shoulder and nuzzled her cheek.

"Guess what!" said Annabel. "I'm the only one in my school who can kiss my elbow!"

"That's wonderful," said Miss Peach, studying the checkerboard. "Gloria, it's your move."

Swiftly, Gloria hopped down on the table and jumped two of Miss Peach's men.

Miss Peach groaned. "Just once! Just once I'd like to beat Gloria at checkers! Annabel, tell Cook to give you a piece of the cake she just baked. It's your favorite. Chocolate."

Annabel stood watching the game, disappointed that her announcement didn't impress them. She wasn't hungry. After a while she slipped away unnoticed and went downstairs. She wanted to take another look at the pieces of Mrs. Vancourt's golden cat.

Even though a bright afternoon sun warmed the pink-and-gold drawing room, Annabel felt uncomfortable in the silence. Alone in this vast room, she sensed that all the toy animals were watching her. Pretending she didn't care, she tiptoed over to the cabinet where Mrs. Vancourt had placed the pieces of the emerald-eyed cat. In the late afternoon light, the lion head on the drawer's round knob looked almost real. For a moment Annabel was afraid to touch it.

"Silly," she said to herself, yanking open the drawer.

Leaning down, she looked all the way to the back. She felt with her hand in the corners. The drawer was empty. The pieces of golden cat that she had seen Mrs. Vancourt place there were gone. There was no cat. Not one piece.

Was the cat in the dollhouse the same cat that had been in pieces a short while ago? Or was it a different one? Rushing back to the nursery, she found Miss Peach and Gloria just finishing up their game.

"Are you sure you didn't take those pieces out to play with them?" asked Miss Peach. "Mrs. Vancourt was very upset this morning when she found them all in a pile in the stair hall. You know you're not to touch her things. Even if they *are* in pieces."

Annabel shook her head. "I didn't. I never do."

"Somebody did," said Miss Peach. "They didn't just move by themselves. But I've fixed them now." She patted the keys that hung on a ring from her belt. "They're locked up tight."

"Where?" asked Annabel.

"Never mind!" Miss Peach laughed. "Where they are, they're safe."

Chapter 7

When no one was looking, Annabel tried flying again, being very careful only to jump off low places. She used all the magic words she knew and even made up some. She kissed her elbows, waving them in the air like wings, but she couldn't fly.

Through the weeks that followed the cat's disappearance in the shop, Annabel waited impatiently for Mr. Cattes to call. She was convinced that the golden cat he had misplaced and the cat in the dollhouse were the same. Every time the phone rang she ran to answer it, but Mr. Cattes never called.

"If only I could search that shop," she told Beatrice, "I'm sure I could find it."

Annabel talked so much about the cat

that Beatrice began to wonder whether it might be real after all.

One day after school, instead of riding the school bus home, Annabel and Beatrice took a bus to town. They walked until suppertime, looking for Mr. Cattes's shop. When they found it, he was locking up. Though he said the emerald-eyed toy had never turned up, he waited while the girls searched the shop and every room of the dollhouse. Reluctantly, Annabel had to admit to Beatrice that if the cat was there, it chose to remain hidden.

Back at the bus stop, tired and disappointed, they sat on the curb to wait. Annabel began to cry. Beatrice leaned against a lamppost, wondering if they were lost.

"It's dark, and I'm hungry," she said. "Are you sure this is the right bus stop? There were lots of people where we got off. You were wrong about the cat. Maybe you're wrong about the bus too."

Annabel wiped her wet cheeks on her coat sleeve. Beatrice made her so mad when she doubted her. "Didn't he say he had a toy gold cat? Didn't he say he'd lost it?"

But she wasn't sure about the bus.

It was very dark now and cold. Beatrice put her arm around Annabel.

At last, far down the silent street, they saw lights. The lights came closer and closer. Expecting the bus, they stood up. But it wasn't the bus. It was a patrol car.

Holding hands, Annabel and Beatrice watched a policeman in a blue uniform get out of the patrol car. Before he could speak, the rear door opened and out hopped Gloria! Right behind her came Mrs. Vancourt and Mrs. Cox.

Annabel and Beatrice were so happy to be found that they didn't mind being lectured all the way home even when they were told that, for going to town without permission, they couldn't go out of their yards after school for a week.

Christmas passed. The snows came, drifting on the terrace, icing the lawns and gardens with frosting as white as a wedding cake's. Using the terrace banisters as a ski slope, Gloria practiced jumps with her new Christmas skis. Annabel tried hers out on a gentler slope. Coasting with Beatrice

took Annabel's mind off flying. The closest
she had come to flying was swooshing
downhill on her red sled with Gloria
perched on her shoulder. When the ice was
black on the reservoir, Gloria taught Annabel to skate. Though Gloria rode around
close to Annabel's ear like a small snow-
ball, she knew how to land on her feet when
Annabel fell down.

Sometimes when the weather was bad,
Annabel roamed about the house alone,
looking for the gold pieces of cat which
Miss Peach had locked away. She tried
drawers and closets and cupboards, but
Miss Peach had hidden the pieces well.
The one place she was never able to search
—which was always kept locked—was the

long chest in the stair hall. It was an old chest, used to store extra linen, carved all over with flowers and faces of mischievous elves. Since Mrs. Vancourt had found the pieces of golden cat in a pile in the stair hall, the chest was a logical place to store them, Annabel figured, and she had tried the lid a dozen times.

One afternoon in late February when the snows were melted and hard rain drummed against the terrace doors, Annabel thought of the cat. Its first visit on that rainy day seemed so long ago. Wandering into the stair hall, she jiggled the chest's carved lid. It was still locked. Kneeling down, Annabel squinted into the empty keyhole. Inside, it was black. She blew into the keyhole, making a little whistle. She tapped on the sides of the chest. She rattled the lid.

"Why don't you try holding your breath?" said a voice from the windowsill.

Annabel whirled around. Crouched on the sill, swishing its golden tail, was the cat! Carefully, she stood up, wanting very much to grab it before it could disappear, not daring to move nearer for fear of frightening it.

"It's all in the breathing," the cat went on. "If you want to open the chest, hold your breath, close your eyes; then breathe out slowly, and you'll get a surprise."

Annabel tried to speak calmly, as though finding the cat again didn't matter. "Holding my breath will only make my face turn red," she said. "I've tried it. I think you have me mixed up with someone else."

"If one of us is mixed up," said the cat, "it isn't I."

Afraid that the cat would disappear if she argued, she decided to try its suggestion. "Promise you won't go away if I close my eyes."

"I'll do no such thing," said the cat haughtily. "I come and go as I like."

"Oh, very well," said Annabel. She took a deep breath and closed her eyes, forgetting that she had no reason for wanting the chest open now.

"Not enough," said the cat. "Shallow breathing leads inevitably to failure. Take a really deep breath."

Annabel sucked in hard.

"Deeper."

Annabel felt like a balloon.

"Now," said the cat, "let it out slowly and wish on the chest."

Annabel felt as if her insides had turned to liquid honey flowing syrupy down a golden river, and as they flowed away she became lighter and lighter until she felt light enough to ride on a butterfly's wing.

She heard a click.

"Now open your eyes," said the cat.

There stood the chest, its lid wide open! But much more incredible, Annabel was floating three feet off the floor!

"I can fly!" she cried.

Immediately she collapsed on the floor with a thump.

The cat laughed.

Annabel rubbed her elbow. "I was flying. I know I was!" she exclaimed. "What happened?"

"Floating isn't flying," said the cat. "Flying takes practice. Floating is only the first step."

Annabel closed her eyes and breathed

deeply again. When she opened them, she was once more floating.

"Keep your breathing regular and even," said the cat. "No shouting until you get the hang of it."

Soon Annabel was able to stretch out flat in the air and roll over. "For months I've tried to fly," she said. "Why couldn't I before?"

"You didn't really think you could," said the cat. "Isn't it amazing the things we don't do simply because we think we can't do them? Wiggle your feet a bit. That's it. Away you go!"

To Annabel's delight, she shot up to the ceiling and sailed down again like a gull riding a fresh breeze.

"Can anyone be a fairy?" she asked. "My friend Beatrice Cox would be very interested—"

"Beatrice Cox is a mortal," said the cat.

"But so am I," said Annabel. Fortunately she was only a foot off the floor when she spoke, for immediately she fell.

The cat began to walk along the windowsill. "Stupid!" it spat at her.

"Don't leave!" called Annabel. "You always leave just when I want to ask you a question."

The cat sat down again. "If you weren't so stupid, you wouldn't need to ask questions."

Annabel decided to overlook its rudeness. "What you mean is if I believe I'm a fairy, I won't fall."

"Don't tell me what I mean," said the cat. "I know what I mean. You're the confused one."

"But if I'm a fairy now, wasn't I a mortal before? Like Beatrice?"

"How could you be?" asked the cat with a sneer. "Your mother is Princess Felicia of the Western Kingdom."

Annabel tingled all over with excitement. "My very own mother is a princess? A fairy princess?" She hugged herself. "So *that's* why I'm a fairy!"

"You're only half," said the cat. "Felicia made the mistake of marrying a mortal named Tippens when she could have chosen any prince in the realm."

Annabel nodded. "Beatrice *said* Tippens didn't sound like a fairy name. So I'm half-mortal like my father and half-fairy like my mother!"

"Unfortunately, yes," said the cat. "A most unsatisfactory arrangement for casting spells or disappearing. I doubt that you'll ever be a really first-rate fairy."

"What about my parents? Do you know where they are?"

"In exile, of course. Felicia's marriage angered her father, the King, so much he exiled her and her mortal spouse to an island far away."

"Someday they will return," said Annabel carefully. That was what Gloria had always told her. "But why can't Gloria talk about them?"

"They wanted you brought up as a mortal," said the cat. "That's why Felicia assigned Gloria to bring you up in the mortal world. Gloria has orders never to tell you that you are part-fairy."

So that was Gloria's secret! No wonder she never talked about Felicia. Suddenly Annabel felt very kindly toward the cat. "And but for you, dear cat, I would have grown up never knowing that I could fly!"

"I understand children," said the cat. "They all want to fly. With practice, you can fly as low as a dragonfly."

"High, you mean," said Annabel. "I want to fly high."

"Anybody can fly high," said the cat. "It's low flying that requires skill. Try hovering over a whitecapped sea without wetting your feet, or following a rabbit's trail up a cliff thick with bayberry without getting a scratch."

Annabel zoomed up to the ceiling and dipped down again, hovering a few inches above the carpet. Then she zoomed under a table. But, trying to maneuver through the legs of a chair, she became hopelessly entangled.

"I see what you mean," she said, getting back into the air. "Don't you think I'm too big to follow a rabbit's trail without getting a scratch?"

The cat didn't answer.

Looking down from the ceiling, Annabel couldn't see it anywhere. She flew down to investigate. On the windowsill, instead of the cat, glittered a neat pile of gold pieces, two of them studded with emeralds.

Thoughtfully, Annabel sifted the golden pieces through her fingers, listening to the clicking noise they made.

"It said it wasn't really a cat," she told herself, sweeping the golden pieces into her hand. Carefully, she placed them in the chest and closed the lid. Now it didn't matter about the cat. The discovery that she was half-fairy was enough. She didn't care if she never saw the cat again.

Chapter 8

Late in the afternoon Mrs. Vancourt came down to the drawing room and immediately rang for Miss Peach.

"There is a large moth flitting about the rooms," said Mrs. Vancourt. "It just passed me in the stair hall."

"If it gets in here, it will eat holes in the tapestries," said Miss Peach. "I'll get a fly swatter."

"You'll need something larger than a fly swatter," said Mrs. Vancourt. "It almost knocked me down. Get some spray."

"That's best," agreed Miss Peach. "Sometimes moths are hard to find."

"This one will be easy. It's red."

"A red moth," mused Miss Peach. "Sounds dangerous."

"Bright red," said Mrs. Vancourt. "Probably a rare species. Save it. The museum may be interested."

Miss Peach nodded. "I'll put it in a bottle."

"It won't fit in a bottle," said Mrs. Vancourt. "You'll need a large box."

Miss Peach thought for a moment. "In the attic there is a fine one, full of old tennis balls. I'll have it brought down right away."

Shaking her head over a moth too large for a bottle, she went off to the kitchen for the bug spray. There she found Cook standing on a stool, swinging a frying pan around her head.

"Watch out for the bird!" shouted Cook. "There was a loose one around here a minute ago! Must have flown down the chimney!"

"Goodness!" said Miss Peach. "If a bird gets in the pantry, it will break all the china. Get down and help me find the butterfly net to catch it."

"It stole five fresh sugar cookies right off the cookie sheet," said Cook, climbing down.

"I didn't know birds liked sugar cookies," said Miss Peach. "What kind of bird was it?"

"A red bird," said Cook.

"A cardinal?"

Cook shook her head. "More like a flamingo. A big bird with legs that hang down."

Miss Peach frowned. "A big red bird?" Then she began to laugh. "Of course! You have nothing to worry about, Cook. It isn't a bird at all! It's a moth."

"A moth? As big as a flamingo? If you didn't see it, how do you know?"

Miss Peach smiled. "Mrs. Vancourt saw it. It almost knocked her down in the stair hall. She said it was a moth, and Mrs. Vancourt can certainly tell the difference between a flamingo and a moth! Help me find the bug spray. I'll take the butterfly net too, just in case."

Cook nodded. "Just in case the moth turns out to be a flamingo."

Armed with the spray and the net, Miss Peach began her search of the downstairs rooms. She found two spiders in the dining room, an overturned chair in the stair hall, and in the small sitting room where Mrs. Vancourt took tea on winter afternoons she found a beetle lost among the blue and white tiles around the fireplace. Just when she was beginning to wonder if the flamingo-moth had flown upstairs, she heard Mrs. Vancourt's shriek from the drawing room.

"Come quick!" shouted Mrs. Vancourt when Miss Peach appeared. "In the corner behind the piano! You take the spray. Give me the net. The moth is bigger than I thought."

"Cook said it was a flamingo," said Miss Peach, squinting toward the piano.

"Cook's an idiot," said Mrs. Vancourt. "Careful now. We don't want to damage its wings. Museums don't like ratty specimens."

Cautiously they approached the piano. Something rustled in the corner. They stopped.

Looking over at Mrs. Vancourt, who carried the butterfly net with both hands, like a spear, Miss Peach whispered, "Do you think we should call the police?"

Mrs. Vancourt glared at her and took another step forward. Whatever it was, bird or moth, it became very quiet.

Then suddenly, with a smashing crash that shook every crystal on the chandelier, the thing swept across the piano keyboard and zoomed across the room.

"Attack! Attack!" shouted Mrs. Vancourt, waving the butterfly net above her head in her charge toward the fireplace.

But Miss Peach stood where she was, both hands held protectively over her head.

"Spray!" ordered Mrs. Vancourt. "I have it cornered. Spray, Miss Peach, as hard as you can!"

Miss Peach kept her eyes shut tightly. "It isn't a moth, Mrs. Vancourt. Spraying won't help. Cook was right. It's a flamingo!"

"Any fool knows we're too far north for flamingos," shouted Mrs. Vancourt. "Don't just stand there. The moth will escape."

"Shall I call the fire department?"

"Miss Peach!" There was a terrible warning note in Mrs. Vancourt's voice.

"Bring the spray immediately! If you will follow my orders, no outside help will be necessary."

Trembling, one hand on her head and one eye shut, Miss Peach advanced with the spray. Stopping beside Mrs. Vancourt, she slowly raised her head to peek at whatever it was they had cornered. With only one eye, she saw the thing hovering near the ceiling in the corner. It definitely wasn't a flamingo. Then she half opened the other eye.

"Oh, my goodness," she said with both eyes wide.

"Give me the spray!" ordered Mrs. Vancourt.

"No, no," said Miss Peach, drawing back. "It won't be necessary. Oh, my goodness, Mrs. Vancourt, put on your glasses! That isn't a moth or a flamingo! All this excitement for nothing. It's only Annabel!"

Mrs. Vancourt fumbled for the gold chain that held her glasses. "What's she doing up there?"

"Eating sugar cookies!" gasped Miss Peach. "She's wearing her new red dress!"

Coming closer, Mrs. Vancourt placed her glasses on her thin nose. "Annabel? Is that you up there?"

Stretched out in midair, Annabel laughed so hard she rolled over. "You should have seen your face, Miss Peach." She giggled. "You were so frightened. Miss Peach was really scared, wasn't she, Mrs. Vancourt?"

Mrs. Vancourt stamped her foot. She was still holding the butterfly net in one hand. "Annabel Tippens! Come down from there! You come down at once!"

"Please, Mrs. Vancourt, it's lovely up here."

"At once, I say! You're dropping cookie crumbs on the carpet. What do you mean by going about frightening people and scattering crumbs through the house?"

Annabel laughed. "Cook thought I was a flamingo."

"Down, I say!"

Slowly Annabel descended until her feet were just three inches off the floor.

Mrs. Vancourt stood frowning, gripping the butterfly net like a banner.

"All the way down!"

Annabel bounced a couple of times, but she obeyed.

"Now. Listen carefully," said Mrs. Vancourt. "No more of that sort of thing in the house. I won't have it. It's too upsetting. You're sure to break something, to say nothing of frightening my guests. As soon as you have apologized to Cook and helped Miss Peach put away the spray and the butterfly net, you are to go to your room. Do you understand?"

"Yes, Mrs. Vancourt."

"You will have dinner in your room and think over what I have said."

"Yes, Mrs. Vancourt." Annabel had learned that when Mrs. Vancourt was upset, it was best to be serious. "May I call Beatrice Cox before dinner?"

"Anything you have to say to Beatrice Cox can wait until tomorrow," said Mrs. Vancourt. She handed the butterfly net to Miss Peach. "Please send Gloria to me immediately, Miss Peach. We'll have tea in the sitting room."

Annabel never knew what Mrs. Vancourt said to Gloria. She was disappointed at not being the first to tell Gloria about flying, but waiting in her room for dinner, she thought of what she would say to Beatrice Cox. Now that she could fly, she could whip over to see Beatrice any time and go right in her window without even knocking on the door. Wasn't Beatrice in for a surprise! And she could fly to school without bothering with the bus. Did fairies need to go to school? She hoped Miss Clemments would let her fly up to the pencil sharpener and out to the water fountain without saying she had to get permission from the Board of Education. When they chose sides, everyone would want her on their team. Someone might even ask for her autograph!

The advantages of being part-fairy were so great that Annabel floated right up to the ceiling just thinking about them. She was stretched out flat over the bureau when Gloria returned.

As soon as she saw Gloria's eyes, Annabel guessed the little dog had been crying. But Gloria looked up at Annabel very

calmly, as though laying out flat over the
bureau was a perfectly normal thing for
Annabel to do.

"Come down, please," she said quietly,
taking her chair by the fire. "Mrs. Vancourt has asked that you not fly in the
house."

"I forgot," said Annabel, sinking down to the stool beside Gloria's chair. "Was Mrs. Vancourt very angry? She thought I was a moth, and Cook thought I was a flamingo!"

Gloria didn't laugh. "When did you see Belinda?" she asked seriously.

Annabel shook her head. "Who is Belinda?"

"The one who told you that you could fly," said Gloria, "who showed you how."

"The gold cat with the emerald eyes told me," said Annabel. "Is her name Belinda?"

"Belinda takes many shapes. She is a powerful fairy and a wicked one. Belinda is my enemy."

Then Annabel told Gloria everything. "When we met, she said she wasn't really a cat. How was I to know she was wicked? She was terribly rude, but she taught me to fly and told me about my mother, Princess Felicia, marrying a mortal. Even though I'll never be a true fairy, being half-fairy is great. With a little more practice I'll be able to fly over to see Beatrice. Watch!"

Before Annabel could take off, Gloria's quiet voice stopped her. "Not in the house."

"Excuse me," said Annabel. "I keep forgetting. Why are you so sad, Gloria? If you are a fairy too like Belinda said, we can have such fun flying together."

Gloria's eyes filled with tears. "It isn't that simple, my dear," she said. "Your mother assigned me a mission, to bring you from the Island of Exile to the mortal world. For reasons I cannot disclose, by allowing Belinda to reach you, I may have failed my mission."

Annabel took Gloria in her arms. "Don't cry," she said. "When my parents return, they will forgive you. Meanwhile everything will go on as before. I'll do as you say. I won't fly in the house; I won't even fly at school if you don't want me to. But please don't say I can't fly at all. I love being a fairy, even part of one. This is the most fun I've ever had."

For a moment Gloria closed her eyes. When she opened them again, she was strangely calm. "Whether to be a fairy or a mortal is a choice you will shortly have to make; you can't remain half one and half the other. Though only you can make the choice, it is my duty to warn you that sometimes a fairy's life is very lonely. Before making a final decision, you should consider the matter carefully." Giving herself a brisk shake, she hopped down from Annabel's arms. "While you stay with Mrs. Vancourt, she will restrict your activities. Of course, you will respect her wishes."

Annabel nodded. "No flying in the house. I'm glad you're a fairy too, Gloria. You're so much nicer than Belinda."

"I am not as powerful," said Gloria, "but Belinda has no heart. Having a heart is my advantage over her. Belinda doesn't understand the power of the heart."

Speaking softly, as though to herself, she said, "Already, with her usual overconfidence, Belinda thinks she has won. My answer will surprise her. Though it will not be easy for me, my heart has told me what I must do. I follow my heart."

Chapter 9

That evening Annabel and Gloria had dinner together by the nursery fire. Later, as though nothing had happened, Miss Peach came in to play checkers with Gloria. Just once, when Annabel was getting ready for bed, she forgot about flying in the house. Unable to reach a fresh tube of toothpaste on the top shelf of the bathroom closet, she zoomed up for it and was back again before she realized what she had done.

Gloria read her a story before she went to sleep. When she kissed Gloria good night, Annabel hugged her close, just like Beatrice Cox hugged her mother. Even though it was going to be wonderful to have a real mother someday, having Gloria was almost as good.

"I love you, Gloria," she whispered.

The little dog nuzzled Annabel's cheek and lay beside her ear on the pillow until Annabel fell asleep.

Outside, a cold night wind whipped up the river long enough to freeze the garden pool and drape the roof with icicles. Then it moved on, leaving the moon to illuminate its art.

In the nursery the fire burned low. For a long while Gloria lay beside Annabel, listening to the night sounds in the house. Deep in the cellar a rat gnawed; Mrs. Vancourt dropped her book and flicked off her light; Miss Peach began to snore. On the stairs, like a night watchman of old, the clock called out the hours.

Then Gloria did a very strange thing. Silently, she slipped out of the nursery and walked down through the quiet dark house to the drawing room. Moonlight streamed from the terrace through the long French doors, stenciling patterns on the carpet. Gloria walked to the door and looked out at the silent, frozen world. She looked down the river to the winking lighthouse and out to sea where two ships passed in the night. She sighed.

Then, hopping on a chair, she opened one of the gold cabinets. She jumped in, stepping over a jade pig no bigger than a thimble, and chose a spot close to Annabel's favorite swan. From there she could see all around the moonlit room and through the glass door to the terrace and the river beyond.

Gloria sat down. She arranged her gold collar, centering the word *GLORIA* neatly at the back of her neck. She licked herself smooth and arranged her tail. Then she took a deep breath and held it.

On the stairs, the clock struck twelve. Slowly the moon moved across the sky, shifting the pools of moonlight on the drawing-room floor—searching the cabinets slowly one by one like a giant spotlight until it reached the shelf where Gloria sat. She was very still. Her tear-filled eyes glittered like diamonds. In the moonlight her white fur turned to gold.

The moon passed on. Gloria didn't move. She wasn't holding her breath any-

more. Like the swan on the shelf beside her, she was still and cold, a glistening toy with a key in her back. Gloria was no longer a little white dog. She had turned herself into a golden dog with diamond eyes!

Next morning when Mrs. Vancourt came into the drawing room, she found

Gloria—a golden toy with a windup key in her back.

"I always knew she wasn't like other dogs," she told Miss Peach, "but this is a peculiar accident. Perhaps I should call the police."

Miss Peach shook her head, turning the golden dog with diamond eyes over and over in her hand. "They wouldn't believe you," she said.

Mrs. Vancourt agreed. "But why did this happen? After all these years. How can we tell Annabel?"

Annabel wasn't in the nursery when Mrs. Vancourt went to wake her. Early in the morning she had flown from the upstairs balcony down to the frozen garden to practice. From the top of a tree where she sat eating an icicle, she watched Mrs. Vancourt approach. Fearing that Mrs. Vancourt would say no flying in the garden as well as in the house, Annabel flew down and pretended to be poking at the ice on the garden pool.

"It's Gloria," Mrs. Vancourt told her sadly. "Something has happened to her.

You'd better come inside."

Hurrying back to the house, Annabel listened to Mrs. Vancourt's story of the little gold dog in the drawing room. "It is the strangest thing that has ever happened in my house!"

"It couldn't be Gloria," insisted Annabel. But remembering how Belinda changed into a golden cat, Annabel entered the house with a sick feeling in her stomach.

Even when Mrs. Vancourt placed the golden dog in her hands and pointed to the name on the collar, Annabel shook her head. Not her Gloria, not her soft warm little friend. "Gloria loves me; she wouldn't leave," she told Miss Peach. "She must be hiding. If we look, we'll find her."

All day, Annabel went through the house. She searched every room. She called and called. All her joy at being able to fly was forgotten.

In the afternoon she came back to the drawing room. Mrs. Vancourt found her standing before the glass case, staring at the gold dog with diamond eyes.

"She does the same tricks Gloria did

when you wind her up," said Mrs. Van-court, "all except the quadruple roll off the mantel into a bowl of water. I suppose that would eventually make her insides rust."

To demonstrate, Mrs. Vancourt wound up the golden dog and placed it on a table. Stiffly, with a ticking noise, the toy began to do Gloria's tricks. Annabel stared. It was like watching a nightmare come true.

Turning away, she ran from the room, crying out, "It isn't Gloria! It can't be!"

Upstairs, she threw herself down in the big chair by the nursery fire, where she and Gloria had spent so many afternoons play-ing and reading together. Alone, she lay there sobbing until Miss Peach brought up her supper tray and put her to bed.

Downstairs, Mrs. Vancourt, as though under a spell herself, sat long after mid-night, winding up the golden toy, watching it go through its tricks over and over again.

When Beatrice Cox called the next day, she was told that Annabel was sick in bed. After that, for many weeks, Dr. Watkins came almost every day.

Because the doctor insisted, Mrs. Van-

court advertised for Gloria in the newspaper, knowing very well that no one had
found a small white dog three inches long
and three inches high. She and Miss Peach
read aloud to Annabel all the letters from
Miss Clemments's class, but for a long time
Annabel was too sick even to notice the get-
well cards which Miss Peach had arranged
on the nursery mantel.

Chapter 10

Spring came slowly. Propped among the pillows of a big chair by the nursery window, Annabel watched the March clouds frolic past the lighthouse. Even when warm fog rolled in from the sea, bringing strange sounds and smells of exotic places beyond the horizon, she felt no desire to join them. Her flying experience seemed so long ago she wondered if she hadn't dreamed it until she remembered that there was no Gloria to hop on her shoulder and nuzzle her cheek or to read aloud to her before bedtime.

Mrs. Vancourt came to the nursery more often. Occasionally she even read to Annabel. Once when Annabel was thinking about Gloria, Mrs. Vancourt patted her hand.

"I miss Gloria too," she said. "You and Gloria have become my family. Even though she is gone, I will care for you always. I am very fond of you, my dear."

In spite of her good intentions, Mrs. Vancourt's busy social season left little time for Annabel. Miss Peach did her best to cheer the child, but spring cleaning added to her usual routine kept her away from the nursery.

When she was strong enough to walk on the upstairs balcony, Annabel sat in the sun, looking down on the lawn, a green quilt patched with buttercups, and on the garden where rabbits and pheasant passed each other on the paths. She wondered if she were strong enough to fly down to join them, but she didn't try. The thought of flying and all that had happened before Gloria disappeared made her feel ill again.

Beatrice Cox was allowed to make brief visits, but because she didn't like sitting still and playing quiet games, Beatrice usually left before visiting time was up. One day Mrs. Vancourt came home just in time to see Beatrice walking around the second-floor balcony railing, balancing herself with outstretched arms.

"It was just a show for Annabel," explained Beatrice when Mrs. Vancourt ordered her down. "I made her laugh."

That Annabel was so sad bothered Beatrice. Funny stories about Miss Clemments and school that Annabel would have shouted over before she got sick now brought only a quiet smile.

"Maybe Gloria went to visit your mother," suggested Beatrice one day when the smell of lilacs filled the house and she and Annabel were on the terrace, playing Old Maid. "She'll come back in time to take you to the beach."

Annabel shook her head. "Gloria loved me. By now, she would have come back if she could. When my mother comes, she'll explain why Gloria left me."

Privately, Beatrice believed Annabel was an orphan, but she asked, "Do you think she'll come soon?"

Annabel frowned. Even Miss Peach was beginning to doubt that she had parents. "Gloria always said my parents would return someday."

Beatrice refused to believe that Gloria could talk, but having orders not to argue with Annabel, she suggested, "Maybe Gloria went to get them."

"There is so much I don't understand," said Annabel, thinking of the gold toy with the diamond eyes in the drawing room. She was able to look at it now without crying. "Ever since that cat told me I was part-fairy and taught me to fly, nothing's been right."

Beatrice shuffled the cards and dealt. She knew Annabel couldn't fly.

"Even if they don't come back," she said, holding up her cards for Annabel to choose one, "even if Gloria has gone forever, Mrs. Vancourt will take care of you."

Annabel chose a card. "She is kind, but she and Miss Peach don't have much time for little girls. I get terribly lonely. When Mrs. Vancourt isn't going out, she's entertaining. Even when Miss Peach finds time to read to me, it isn't like having a real mother. Gloria was like a real mother."

Beatrice covered her smile with her cards. Annabel had the wildest ideas.

Gloria couldn't have been like a real mother!

"When my parents come," Annabel continued, "I won't be lonely anymore. I hope they will be as nice as yours. I want my father to toss me in the air and play, and I want my mother to comfort me and hold my hand and tuck me in at night. You're lucky, Beatrice."

Beatrice thought for a moment. "Parents are okay," she admitted, "but, Annabel, if you ever get any, you'll have to forget this stuff about being a fairy and flying. Everybody believes in fairies, but believing you *are* one—well!—I know my father wouldn't put up with that one minute!"

After Beatrice went home, Annabel wandered out to the kitchen. It was Cook's afternoon off, and the refrigerator's quiet hum was the only sound. On the kitchen table sat the big glass cookie jar, half full of sugar cookies. Unscrewing the lid, Annabel reached in and helped herself.

Just then the newspaper Cook had left on the table began to crackle. Something was moving it. Annabel drew back, hoping

it wasn't a mouse. *Rustle, flutter, blam!*
Like a rocket, the something came bursting
through the front page, landing squarely
on the table in front of Annabel. She
blinked. Nonchalantly, as though it had
never been away, the golden cat with the
emerald eyes looked up at her.

"Belinda!"

"You know my name?" The cat walked
over to the cookie jar and sat down. "Gloria
must have told you. Poor thing, she was always jealous of me. You know, she didn't
want you and me to become friends."

"You're wicked," said Annabel loyally,
remembering that Belinda was Gloria's
enemy. "You're not supposed to talk to me."

The cat swished its tail. "Jealousy drove
Gloria to say unkind things about me. Have
I ever hurt you, my dear? Didn't I tell you
about being a fairy and teach you to fly?"

"You weren't supposed to. When I
learned to fly, Gloria was very unhappy.
That's when she went away. Do you know
where she went?"

"Isn't she in the drawing-room cabinet?
That golden dog in there wears her collar."

"That isn't Gloria," said Annabel. She was sure of it.

"Suit yourself," said the cat, "but it appears to me that Gloria tried one trick too many and got stuck. She was always showing off. What about you? Have you been flying?"

"No," said Annabel. "I've been sick."

"Too bad," said the cat. "Flying's such fun. If you're feeling better, why don't we spin out to the lighthouse and back?"

"You mean now? Fly? Way out there?"

The cat laughed. "Well, I'm not much of a swimmer. What's the fun of knowing how to fly if you can't go to exciting places? Tomorrow, if you're feeling up to it, we might go up to Canada."

Annabel had always wanted to go out to the lighthouse, but she didn't trust Belinda. Any enemy of Gloria's had to be her enemy too. Without taking her eyes off the cat, Annabel reached into the glass cookie jar for another cookie.

Paying no attention, the cat sat there swishing its tail.

Carefully, Annabel reached again toward the cookie jar, all the while smiling at Belinda. This time, before the golden cat could suspect her movement, Annabel grabbed it and threw it in the cookie jar. In a twinkling she screwed the lid on tight.

"Now for a few questions!" she exclaimed, peering through the glass jar at Belinda.

The cat stood on the pile of cookies, looking back at her. Suddenly realizing what Annabel had done, she bared her little teeth and screamed.

"Quiet!" commanded Annabel. "I'll let you out when you answer my questions. Why did you tell me I was a fairy and teach me to fly when you knew Gloria had orders never to tell me?"

Again the cat screamed at her, its emerald eyes rolling crazily.

"Answer me," warned Annabel. From past experience, she was worried that it might collapse into pieces and disappear. But, for all its powers, it now appeared to be her prisoner. "Why did you teach me to fly?"

Steam shot out of the cat's ears. It made terrible faces, all the while rising slowly to the top of the jar.

Bravely, Annabel picked up the cookie jar and shook it. Inside, there was a wild scramble of cat, cookies, and crumbs.

Belinda shrieked. "Let me out! You're getting sugar all over me. If you want me to talk, let me out!"

Annabel gave the jar another good shake.

Again the cat shrieked. "Sugar destroys me! Stop that shaking!"

Annabel watched the cat rise again above the pile of broken cookies, brushing itself free of crumbs. It sat under the lid on nothing, its little emerald eyes flashing fire.

"Stupid!" it spat at her. "When I taught you to fly, I was trying to help you. Gloria doesn't understand children. She wanted to keep you mortal forever, when everybody knows being a fairy is much more fun!"

Suspecting the cat was holding back part of the truth, Annabel picked up the jar again.

"Wait!" cried the cat, going up and down in the jar like an elevator.

"The truth this time," warned Annabel.

"I always tell the truth," said Belinda, again settling near the lid, "but there *is* more. When the King exiled your parents, that meddling Gloria intervened. She begged him for their release until he promised to set them free if his daughter's firstborn child became a mortal by the time it was seven."

"Was I the firstborn?"

"Why else would Gloria have brought you here to the mortal world to live for seven years in ignorance of your powers? It was the only way she could save Felicia since she had given the King her word never to tell you of his promise. Of course, once you discovered fairy powers, you would be made to choose between being a mortal or a fairy. Gloria knew the King believed no fairy child would give up its fairy powers to be a mortal—she knew her only hope of saving Felicia was to trick you into believing you were a mortal. Then when the seven years were up, Felicia and her mortal husband would be free. It was terribly unfair of her, don't you think?"

Annabel frowned. The cat talked so fast she wasn't sure what to think, but she kept remembering that Gloria had said it was her enemy.

"I came to help you," it said. "If you'll open this silly jar, we can still fly out to the lighthouse. What wonderful things I can teach you! How to turn yourself into a gull or a butterfly. Would you like to ride on a camel? Or an elephant? Or swing with the monkeys through the top of the jungle? We can explore the oceans with the flying fish, make snowballs on the tops of the highest peaks, and ride with the winds into the stars."

All the adventures that Annabel had dreamed of when she was trying to be a fairy came rushing back to her. She began remembering how it had felt to swoop through the house, zooming up and down the stairs, and to take off from the roof to land in the garden. What fun she had that morning—before Mrs. Vancourt discovered Gloria in the drawing-room cabinet!

Suddenly remembering that morning, Annabel's heart began to ache. In spite of what Belinda had said, she knew Gloria did not intend her harm. For a moment she sat thinking. "And if I don't go with you, if I stay here and become a mortal forever and ever, will my parents be free?"

"You can't be serious," said Belinda. "What a price to pay for parents you can't even remember! My dear, on their little island they not only have everything they need, they also have each other."

Annabel thought some more. Gloria had said Belinda had no heart, that she didn't understand the power of the heart. Belinda couldn't love.

"You'll never be able to fly again," warned the cat. "Once you make the choice, it's made forever."

Through the window Annabel could see gulls wheeling above the cliffs, fishing for their dinner. "When night comes in the jungle and I'm tired of swinging through the trees with the monkeys or riding on an elephant's back and I get scared, who will hold me close? And when I get sick, who will hold my hand or tuck me in or kiss me good night? You make a fairy's life sound very grand, but Gloria said it's lonely sometimes. I don't like being lonely."

"Pish, posh," said the cat. "You'll be too busy to get lonely."

Remembering that the cat was Gloria's enemy, Annabel began to unscrew the cookie-jar lid. "As much as I would enjoy being a fairy occasionally, for everyday, I'd rather be a plain little girl with parents, like Beatrice Cox."

Opening the jar, she placed the cat back on the table. She even dusted some sugar off its back.

The cat backed away beyond reach. "You won't be able to fly—even up the stairs," it warned. "For the rest of your life you'll have to climb thousands and thousands of stairs."

Annabel didn't care. She smiled. "If I can have a father who will toss me in his arms and play and a mother who will kiss me when I come home from school and fix me milk and cookies, then I don't mind climbing a million stairs. Tell your king my mind's made up. If I can have my parents back, I'll give up being a fairy forever and ever."

Belinda's golden face slowly turned to glowing red-hot metal. She clawed the table; steam shot from her ears. "Stupid!" she screeched.

Watching this performance, Annabel wondered if Belinda would fall apart before her eyes. In a moment Belinda's face cooled to a tarnished gray. Then, without another word, she turned away and disappeared over the edge of the table.

Chapter 11

Going up the back stairs from the kitchen,
Annabel almost collided with Miss Peach.
At the same moment the doorbell began to
ring.

"No one's expected," said Miss Peach,
hurrying to answer the urgent ringing.
"Let's hope Mrs. Vancourt hasn't invited
guests and forgotten to tell me!"

Curious, Annabel followed her to the
front hall.

The moment Miss Peach touched the
knob the door sprang open as though by
magic, almost upsetting her, admitting with
the ocean breeze the strangest couple
Annabel had ever seen. The man was
young and tall, with hair the color of honey-
suckle and eyes that twinkled like blue

water in the sun. The woman, whom Annabel took to be his wife, was beautifully dressed in blue clothes that floated around her like soft feathers. Her pretty blond head came up only as high as his waist, for she was not much taller than Annabel.

"May I ask who's calling?" said Miss Peach, so rattled by the strange couple's entrance she forgot to close the door.

The man and his wife exchanged looks full of laughter. They seemed to share a hilarious secret. Before the man could answer, his little wife, seeing Annabel, started to drift toward her like a beautiful blue butterfly.

The moment Annabel felt the woman's touch she guessed who she was. The silky cheek against hers, the warm embrace, the comforting hand against her hair could only belong to her mother.

"The name," said the man, "is Tippens. Mr. and Mrs. Thomas Tippens."

Realizing all of a sudden what was happening, Miss Peach gasped. "Annabel! They've come back!"

The spell was broken! Annabel hugged

her mother. Then her father gave her a big kiss, swinging her up in the air exactly like Mr. Cox swung Beatrice. Annabel laughed. She could tell her father was very strong.

"My very own!" she kept saying over and over through happy tears. "My very own parents!"

Miss Peach, who said it was just like in the movies, began to cry too, and Mr. and

Mrs. Tippens joined in. The four of them stood there crying until Miss Peach managed to tell Annabel to take them into the drawing room while she called Mrs. Vancourt and fixed tea.

Seating her parents on the drawing-room sofa, Annabel climbed into her father's lap. He lent her his handkerchief to blow her nose. It was difficult to believe her mother was a real fairy princess. Reaching over, she gave her mother's small hand a soft squeeze. "Gloria said you would return. If only she could have told me about the spell, I would have broken it long ago."

"Nothing else could have kept us from you," said her father. "We wanted to be with you more than anything."

Mrs. Tippens lifted Annabel's hand to her cheek, setting in motion the soft tendrils of her blue gown. "Gloria is our dearest friend. We have her to thank for bringing us all together again."

"I thought she loved me too much to go away," said Annabel.

"She loved you most of all," said her mother.

Mr. Tippens nodded. "It was because she loved you so much that she went away. Leaving you was the only way she knew to help you. Felicia, explain it to her."

Mrs. Tippens touched her eyes with a handkerchief as soft as a silver cobweb. "When our enemy, the wicked fairy Belinda, told you that you were a fairy and taught you to fly, she believed you would choose to be a fairy forever and ever, destroying completely our chances to escape from the Island of Exile."

Annabel began to understand. "Was that why Gloria was so sad? But why did she leave me? I missed her so much I got sick. When she didn't come back, I wished for you to return. I wanted parents like other little girls. I wanted someone to love me."

Her mother nodded. "That is exactly what Gloria planned. Though it was terribly hard to leave you, she hoped that with no one to love you and give you a mother's care you might change your mind about wanting to be a fairy forever and ever. Of course, she was forbidden to tell you about the spell. She could only hope you would break it in time. Fortunately, you were able to force the information from Belinda."

"And Gloria?" asked Annabel, climbing into her mother's arms. "That gold dog isn't really Gloria, is it? Has she gone away forever?"

Her mother smoothed Annabel's hair. "Gloria had to return to the kingdom of the fairies. If all goes well, she will be free to visit us soon—before she begins her stage career."

"Hurray!" shouted Annabel, clapping her hands.

At that moment Mrs. Vancourt entered the room, followed by Miss Peach with the tea tray.

Annabel made the introductions.

"Tippens?" said Mrs. Vancourt, putting on her glasses to peer at Annabel's parents. "When Annabel learned to fly, Gloria told me who Annabel's mother was, but she didn't identify her father. Thomas, why are you using that name? You know very well what your name is!"

"Of course," said Mr. Tippens. "I

changed it in anger years ago."

"Well, you change it right back," said Mrs. Vancourt. "And that suit—a good tweed when it was new. It doesn't fit anymore. Can't your wife wave a wand or something and make it the right size?"

Mr. Tippens smiled warmly, taking her hand. "Are you glad to see me?"

Annabel stared at her father and Mrs. Vancourt. Listening to their conversation, she realized they had met before. Amazed, she watched Mrs. Vancourt, like a queen bestowing favors, kiss her father's forehead. Then, leaning down, Mrs. Vancourt pressed a thin cheek against her mother's soft one. Annabel had never seen her greet anyone so familiarly before.

Smiling kindly, Mrs. Vancourt spoke in a strained voice. "Welcome to our family, my dear. Thomas has no doubt told you that I am his mother."

Annabel wondered if she were dreaming. "His mother?"

"His mother!" shrieked Miss Peach, who had not recognized him. "Tommy! You've come home!"

Astonished, Annabel watched Miss Peach throw her arms around Mr. Tippens and dance him around the drawing room. Turning to Mrs. Vancourt, she asked, "Does that mean you are my grandmother?"

Mrs. Vancourt nodded. "Provided you don't go flying about. The Vancourts *don't* fly."

Annabel wondered how Mrs. Vancourt could remain so calm through the excitement until she saw her grab the back of a chair to steady herself and dab at the corner of her eye with her handkerchief when she thought no one was looking. Poor Mrs. Vancourt. She was just as happy as Miss Peach to have her son return. But, unlike

Miss Peach, she didn't know how to show it.

As soon as Mrs. Vancourt sat down, Annabel climbed up on her lap and gave her a big kiss. "I'm so glad you are my grandmother," she said. "If you don't mind, I'm going to give you a kiss every single day forever and ever."

And before Mrs. Vancourt could express disapproval, Annabel climbed down and ran to her mother. "I just can't wait another moment," she told her. "Now that you're back and I know we're going to see Gloria again, I've just got to phone Beatrice Cox!"

Format by Phoebe Amsterdam
Set in 14/16 Egmont
Composed by American Book-Stratford Press, Inc.
HarperCollins Publishers